Soul Soap

Juan Manuel Rodriguez Caamano

Chapter 1

In the year 2070, humans found the most efficient way to coexist. We were able to train exemplary citizens, thanks to a specialized division of labor, the use of technology, and we developed an almost perfect system of administration of justice that was implemented throughout the world. It was a complex task, but thanks to two impeccable actions it was possible to achieve it: communication between the beings of the planet and the innovative process of social reinsertion of criminals, popularly known as *Soap of Souls.*

For centuries, we have tried all sorts of methods to inhibit inappropriate behavior. From torture in the Holy Inquisition to the electric chair. These methods were voted at the World Assembly of Inhumane and Inefficient Leaders. On July 7, 2070, behaviors of physical abuse in people who commit an offense were abolished. The death penalty became an example of barbarism that could never be repeated.

At the end of 2069, the last prison systems in the world were closed and those that persisted were located in the poorest countries, where creating spaces for the purification of souls represented a strong investment of financial and human resources. Fortunately, the white flag was decreed on December 27 of that year and all prisons and rehabilitation systems were abolished and the Purification System was approved for all citizens who committed a serious crime. Minor illegalities were compensated and sanctioned with social work to help improve the system.

This achievement began to be forged in the year 2052, when a Mexican scientist named Ignacio González Sánchez, graduated from the Industrial Engineering career of the Universidad de Sotavento, carried out sophisticated studies in all areas of science to discover a viable alternative, since despite global efforts, the signs of criminality were increasing, but two components continued to be acted on, up to now in an unsatisfactory manner: behavior and the mind.

It was at the end of 2060, when Dr. González demonstrated the existence of that intangible element that we called soul for a long time. All the religions had told us about that part of the body, but no one had been able to describe it or know its location.

The investigations not only proved the presence of a soul in each human being, but also, it was possible to understand its operation, the existence of the previous records encoded there, and most importantly: its direct relationship with the crimes committed on Earth. . Finally, after determining its existence and functioning, the next step was to establish a way to alter its state and bring the damaged individuals of their soul to ideal states of human coexistence.

After many centuries of unnecessary punishment and penance, of failed psychiatric treatments, which increased the rates of violence and crime in the world, science finally managed to solve one of the most worrying problems in the history of homo sapiens. The confinements tried to modify behavior based on fear, and complex medicines: the mind. The new research question to be answered with the newly discovered knowledge was: how to purify the soul? With groups of associated scientists in each continent of the world and sharing the findings in a fluid and constant way, the hypothesis that responded to the problem presented in the world was forged. They hoped to find an ideal alternative to have a harmonious planet and preserve the species for millions of more years.

From 2064 to 2066, a record time, a soul purification system began to be implemented experimentally in volunteers from all over the world, a treatment consisting of mild electric shocks, right in the middle part of the chest, where an organ is located at the which many owe the name of thymus.

In millions of citizens, treatments with different frequencies and voltages were tested to establish a standardized process that would cleanse the soul and be able to reintegrate criminals into society, but not before having completed a period of social work. None of the volunteers showed any problem with any of the experimental treatments that filled the planet with optimism.

It was also discovered that by purifying the soul it was not necessary to work on people's minds, since when working on that essence of each human being, bad or good memories were forgotten. It was like being born again in moral concepts for the rehabilitated, but with the basic knowledge acquired previously.

From there, training was carried out for a couple of months, where the desired behaviors were established in each individual and love of teamwork was encouraged in favor of a better environment. It was amazing to see serial killers become change agents, civilized people who could coexist with others and work selflessly for their community. It seemed like a dream come true for the pacifists. As an indirect result and without scientific evidence to prove it, the world had calmed down. Conflicts between nations were decreasing as if a foam reached them, subtracting grudges.

From 2066 to 2067, the legal framework for the application of soul purification treatments was established. The treatment times and the types of social work that the rehabilitated would carry out were specified, according to the crime and its magnitude. The current legislation would be modified annually, depending on the results to perfect it.

Episode 2

The rest of the world showed amazing results in all aspects of life, despite the fact that the justice system was newly implemented.

Violent practices were gradually eradicated, allowing cities of vast and beautiful nature to detonate tourism. It happened with developing countries in Latin America and Africa, which enjoy incomparable landscapes. For centuries, economic models based their strategy on the investment of capital goods to produce more. However, by serendipity they realized that, looking for a perfect model for the administration of justice, they found a trigger in the development of the towns, not only economic, but also social and cultural. People could live happily and enjoy every corner of the planet with less risk.

They began to enjoy beautiful landscapes in Tierra del Fuego or in the heights of Bolivia. They met species of animals in their habitat in the most beautiful natural places on the African continent.

The world seemed like a utopia in the year 2070. It was a dream come true for the inhabitants of Earth. And while they enjoyed that peace and tranquility, there was a place where intense work was done to rehabilitate criminals and the necessary inputs were also produced to reduce poverty and hunger indices.

The place chosen for *Soap of Souls* had to be a place away from civilization, where people could carry out their work, without mundane distractions. The tasks to be carried out were development projects for the world population, not for a specific country, but a general contribution, a task with which a feeling of belonging would be generated and they could be proud to add to reduce the problems of humanity.

The cold of Everest would be the place to atone for their guilt and in record time return to society, renewed and with a spirit of teamwork and cooperation. They were separated from the rest of the planet, but they were treated as human beings, with all the labor rights required and in excellent organizational climate conditions to carry out their work, although a minority, where those affected by some of the crimes of the purified were located. he was against giving them that opportunity and treating them as humans for all the heinous actions they committed before they were sentenced to *Soap of Souls.*

The main world need was for food. Attempts by large organizations to eradicate hunger had been in vain. Few people selflessly contribute to this issue, and for that reason, *Jabón de Almas* was part of the solution, not only for social reintegration, but also for the serious food crisis in the world. For this reason, most of them dedicated themselves to that turn. The goal was to be self-sustaining and that no human being go hungry.

Chapter 3

An extensive reserve had been created, near the highest mountain in the world, Everest, a wonderful place, with an extraordinary view and all the necessary tools to supply the world with basic needs: water and food at will.

It was a concentration camp, but totally opposite to those created by the Germans in World War II, where the inhabitants were expiated who had to fulfill their work tasks for the benefit of the world community. They always sought to have the optimal conditions so that each "washing", as the residents were commonly called, could develop all their talent and their physical health was ideal. They had a regimen designed by nutrition experts, graduates of the best universities in the world, including the Universidad Istmo Americana, where Dr. González taught Research. They slept their eight hours a day and their health was evaluated every month by doctors in a camp supervised by the Leeward University School of Medicine. Their lost souls, at some point, became pure and dedicated to serving others. Until then the system had worked perfectly.

Being there created a stigma for those purified by their criminal past, however, with this alternative, violence and crime in the world were reduced to rates close to zero. Perhaps that negative vision of the place also helped to ensure appropriate behavior in the inhabitants of the world. Despite any negative opinion, the residents of that limbo were the happiest on the planet, and no flash of violence would ever cross their minds again.

It was understandable that the rest of the planet's inhabitants did not have access to *Soap of Souls* or to the people there so as not to contaminate the successful transformation process.

There were indicators of each part of the process, and it only remained to wait a few years to see what it was like, in its last stage, the departure of the "purified" to return to society.

The immense field was divided into smaller stations, with specific tasks to achieve better work specialization. At the entrance to *Jabón de Almas , there was* a small station called General Administration, where any management issue, inputs, outputs, inputs, products, problems, assignments, controls, efficiency and human resources was resolved.

One winter day a woman came from a remote place in the south pole, Megan. For her the cold would not be an obstacle. He was in charge of supporting the administration of *Jabón de Almas resources.* She was sent by the World Parliament to advise the project. Her credentials were among the best in the world, which is why they decided to send her to contribute her knowledge in favor of Earth. He could not enter the stations, but he did communicate constantly with them. Sometimes I would get as far as that wall and I could see some of the expiated working hard, especially those who dedicated themselves to harvesting in that land for almost the entire day, to try to supply the largest number of people in the world with top quality grains. .

Others carried out health support activities or offered themselves for complex studies in that same area, generating, with these experiments, the solution to many diseases that afflicted the planet. There were many stations, with thousands of "purified", as they called the residents of the stations. The first two were dedicated to the most essential, food.

There was a young man, Bastián, who worked like a machine from very early until nightfall. His task was simple, but his commitment was so great that he wanted to never rest in order to produce more and make more families happy. His work proved vital to humanity and the place.

Chapter 4

The first and most important station was the water station. There was no other compound more important to life than water.

Most of it was for human consumption, but vast fields were also made fertile with state-of-the-art technology and worked seasonally by purifiers based on that water.

In this way, a world, with billions of people suffering from hunger, became a minority of approximately six percent of the world's population, an incredibly exponential advance in just a couple of years. This justice system not only had a strong impact on the world's crime rates, but also on the coexistence and development of peoples.

There, in Station 1, Bastián worked hard, paying a penance for a sin he was unaware of. It couldn't even go through his mind to harm someone, on the contrary, he was a pure altruist.

Station 2 was located in front of the first, and they were the only two that came together. All the other terminals were kilometers away, one from the other, but terminals 1 and 2 had a common flank where they went from purifying water in huge dams to a clean electricity production system, which was in charge of Station 2 and the citizens who took care of it.

To avoid emotional relationships, each volunteer was known as the "purified" and not prisoners to prevent them from learning about their past. They had their badge, with their station number, the first letter of their name, the number with which they arrived at that place and the date they did so.

The inmates barely exchanged words at each station, and between different terminals it was even more difficult. It seemed that they had lost the desire to socialize. They were only dedicated to working to contribute to humanity.

That winter, the dam reached a very low level. Climate change, which began decades ago, caused record negative indicators. It was then that the experts from each station had to meet and stop work for a day.

The intersection of the station was stations one and two, which was known by the inmates as station one point five. Bastián rested there, after an intense day. Sometimes he would make sixteen-hour shifts to try to supply as many people as possible. In every extra hour worked, he saw millions of people who could improve their health in the world. He sat exhausted on a wooden box that marked Station 1 on one side and Station 2 on the other. The cold that day was not so intense and you could smell winter on the frozen leaves of the trees.

A few minutes later, Megan sat down on the other side of the box, at the edge of Station 2.

"We'll have vacations apparently," Megan said.

- I don't like vacations. I just want to work, non-stop, to improve the world - Bastián said, with some anger, for Megan's comment.

- Seriously, do you care too much about millions of people you don't know? Megan lashed out.

- Wouldn't you worry?

"Sure," Megan answered uncertainly.

Then, Bastián questioned her:

- You don't seem very convinced. If helping others is not what you most want, then what are you doing here?

Bastián stood up from the wooden bench and began to slowly withdraw.

Megan was answering:

- I am responsible for ensuring that the entire process of purification and generation of electrical energy works optimally. I spent my whole life studying to put into practice what I learned at university. You think I would be here, if I didn't think that the most important thing is to help others.

"Having so many titles or knowledge doesn't make you a good person," Bastián told him, already withdrawing completely, visibly annoyed.

Megan sat there without turning to see him, and some tears of pain and hate flowed from her eyes.

Chapter 5

They did not meet again until that day when Megan vanished before their eyes, due to a decompensation and the exhaustion of many hours of work.

Before picking her up and seeing her on the sand, Bastián remembered the unpleasant words they had exchanged when they met, however, he was a citizen committed to humanity, so he held her in his arms and took her to where the medical services were. from Station 1 who were the only ones Bastián knew.

Megan spent a large part of the morning, between rigorous medical examinations, the application of serum and some vitamins, until she came to.

Shortly after, Bastián entered his room and trying to forget a bit about the grudge he held for that unfortunate meeting they had in the past, he told him:

- How are you? You fainted and I brought you to my station because I didn't know where your infirmary was.

- And since you are very altruistic, you ran to save me - Megan replied, with a sarcastic tone.

- Are you still with that? I thought you had already forgotten that difference.

- How can I forget it if you do more for the world moving and sowing hundreds of grains than I do creating the technology for the two seasons to work.

- Look, I'm not going to argue with you, especially now that you need to rest. It is obvious that you do more than me. If you want to humiliate me, go ahead, but the difference is that I do it out of love for others and you do it out of love for your work. That's the difference between you and me - Bastián answered, quite annoyed, not considering that Megan was in bed.

- The difference between you and me? Megan said. Someday I'll ask you that same question and we'll see what you answer, but in the meantime, I owe you my health. So the least I can do is buy you a coffee at our station, the only one that has this elixir in the whole place.

Bastián was tempted to refuse, but he adored coffee and despite not liking it at all, Megan couldn't help but see something inexplicable in his eyes, a shine that when she wanted to bring out the worst in him and get upset, on the contrary, she would calm down and I felt a little empathy with her.

- Only because the last time I tried that elixir was three years ago, when I entered the station to celebrate the end of my training - he said with a joking smile -, because, to tell the truth, the company is not that pleasant. Do not believe, we can be a great team. Everything is for the benefit of humanity.

He got as close as possible to the bed in the room full of monitors, slowly shook her right hand, and she returned the gesture immediately:

- Is it okay with you on your day off? What day did you choose?

- I chose to work every day without rest - It seemed that Bastián had too heavy a load to relieve, because he did not allow himself to rest for a single day. So I can choose any day and, to be honest, since you mentioned the word coffee I can't stop imagining and feeling that delicious aroma. I would love to be out tomorrow, if you are discharged today and if you can, otherwise it's up to you to decide the day, but don't let it last this week because I'm dying to try caffeine.

- Say no more, in fact, the doctor said that in a couple of hours I could leave. I'll see you tomorrow at nine in the morning in the station cafeteria. Take my card so you can have access without any problem.

Chapter 6

The station cafeteria was a very nice place. It looked like a café in Paris because of the tapestries on its walls and the dark wood of its furniture. It had a nice view of the lake that fed the dam and that gave it a more special touch. In summer, beautiful and leafy trees were appreciated, now covered with winter snow. The decoration of beautiful flowers in pots, with cute glass and wood designs, created a very pleasant feeling.

Bastián arrived half an hour before. He didn't remember having ever dated someone, although this meeting with Megan he didn't consider it like that, but rather as a friendship, between two co-workers, trying to smooth things over and work together to leave a legacy for the new generations. He was proud of each day of the work he did.

He ordered a latte to calm his nerves about seeing Megan again. He didn't understand why, if their brief encounters hadn't been pleasant. It was that green tone of her look that he liked the most in her, whether it was with anger or sweetness, that brightness was too much for Bastián.

They talked for hours about the moments each one lived at their stations and laughed out loud at the funny anecdotes that each one had gone through, such as when Bastián took the wrong terminal to go to work. He would order over and over cup of coffee and feel relief in each taste of those roasted beans, to the point where he felt the commitment to return to work. He tried to say goodbye to Megan, but her question made him forget about his work for a moment.

- I think it's time to go back to work – Bastián said as he slowly got up from his chair.

- What do you remember before living at the station, Bastián? – She responded immediately and he sat down again and thought in silence for a couple of seconds.

- The same as everyone: nothing.

- But, what did they tell you?

Bastián fell silent, trying to remember like when someone is unconscious and doesn't remember anything and goes back and forth trying to force his mind to review the past. And suddenly the words began to come out of him:

- That an accident damaged my cerebral cortex and I couldn't remember anything from my past life. So the best option to continue doing what I liked the most was to enlist in a station to work for the good of humanity.

- And did you find it attractive to work in this place, away from the rest of the world?

- Not to you? Most of the people that I have asked that, they tell me that it was the best thing that could have happened in their lives. Do not you believe it?

- Of course I do. Stop thinking that I'm heartless –she told him smiling-, but you haven't thought that maybe there were people who appreciated you before you came here and they probably miss you.

- When I woke up from the accident I didn't know anyone, so I can't imagine that. In addition to the fact that in most cases they told us that we did not have family or that we had probably lost it in the accident. There was no point in reliving those tragic moments and all that remained was to look forward.

- You're right: now this is our world, our new family and for which we must seek.

Bastián began to feel calmer, although the only type of family relationship that would please him, at some point with Megan, is for her to be his wife.

- Did they tell you something different, Megan?

- They told me exactly the same thing – she replied with her face visibly sad; her eyes sparkled trying to avoid a tear. He seemed to remember something, but his memory blocked it. I think I should go back to work. It is a difficult day. I was happy to greet you. Any day you have available, you can come to the station cafeteria and we will drink an espresso, courtesy of the director of Station 2.

"Well, if it were up to me, I would come every week to collect that espresso," Bastián told her, wanting to see her again for more than just another coffee.

- Well, come every week at this time and we'll talk, it'll be a nice custom for the start of the week - she proposed winking at him, and she got up from the table without formally saying goodbye, just took the band where her access card to the place hung.

Chapter 7

At first, Bastián thought that Megan's offer to talk every Tuesday at seven twenty in the morning was just a courtesy, but there was nothing to lose by checking it out, besides that this memory generated great emotion in him. That fusion of the aroma of coffee with the perfume on her skin was something she had not experienced, and her gaze along the horizon over the lagoon made a unique landscape.

Seven thirty-five struck and Bastián was about to leave the place when he saw the cafeteria door open. A beautiful silhouette carried with her a document with information about the operation of Station 2. Megan used it to pretend that she was consulting some matters of her work and not look like an idiot planted in case he didn't show up for the appointment.

She was very surprised when, upon entering and seeing the empty cafeteria, someone gently patted her beautiful back.

- You arrive very punctual; It's barely seven thirty-five- Megan said barely recovered from the surprise. She looked beautiful, always dressed in white. Being the director allowed her to dress differently from others. I was thrilled to think that it hadn't just been a courtesy to her weekly coffee treat.

- I already wanted to see you – Bastián let go at first. I mean, I already wanted to enjoy that delicious coffee that they prepare here.

- I also wanted this Tuesday to come back to fight with you- Megan replied laughing and infecting Bastián with her sarcasm.

They sat down to drink coffee accompanied by delicious pancakes. They spent two hours talking about their lives at the station. When they were together they forgot the whole world and their occupations. Time and space did not matter. This is how the second date went. The most contrasting thing was that after a turbulent beginning of their friendship, they now anxiously awaited the arrival of Tuesdays.

- It's my turn to pay the bill - Bastián told him trying to correspond to his first invitation.

- Okay! But I invite the next one, okay? - Megan's smile made Bastián blush until he was silent - and so we go: one you, one me.

- Will there be next? - Bastián thought aloud, with the desperation of someone who feels lost what he wants too much, although he knew instantly that it was a silly question.

- If you don't want it, no - she said with her characteristic smile.

- Of course I want it.

- Well do not say more. See you here next Tuesday.

They both parted with a kiss on the cheek. It was the first time he felt the smoothness of her skin. He opened the door for her to let her out and kept looking at her all the way down the corridor that led her to her station. In her wake, she left the trail of her new perfume and in the background the relaxed music from the cafeteria permeated. At times he waited for that classic romantic scene of turning back and colliding glances, but Megan never turned around, on the contrary, she walked quickly and disappeared at the end of the road.

Tuesdays were immensely happy for both of them. They talked about so many things, from the subtlest things about work to the deepest things about their lives, thoughts and expectations.

They began to wish for what up to now they had not done for several years of their life in the stations, a normal life. The one they knew existed far from that place, with travel, home, children, social coexistence and self-realization.

Chapter 8

That Tuesday, March 7, was not one more. With the confidence of more than three months sharing coffee every week, Bastián tried to tell Megan what he felt.

They did not remember anything from their past life, but a small feeling grew every Tuesday in their hearts. The simple sip of a cup of coffee, with the presence of the other caused a boil of endorphins in their bodies, a unique and indescribable happiness for both. They seemed to know each other forever. In their few differences, instead of debate, they intertwined their points of view so as not to fight, but to seek homogeneous points of view.

Despite his long talks on Tuesdays, Bastián did not rest that day. He came straight to catch up on work. He should not neglect his commitment to the world for anything or anyone.

There was something that both were unaware of, for obvious reasons, each of the "purified", depending on the seriousness of their crimes in their lives prior to the cleansing of their soul, had a minimum sentence of one year. They weren't the kind of sentences where you spent your life locked in a cell. It was a short time to contribute to the world and remunerate society a little, because in theory they would never commit crimes again. Their souls were pure. That was the desired goal with the Purification Program. That was the theme of that Tuesday. Winter had hardly passed, but the low temperatures continued. They drank coffee to excess to try to counteract the cold that was felt in the cafeteria.

- And why are you interested in returning to the world and leaving the station? If you have told me that your life is to work to improve the world- she questioned him.

Bastián was silent for a few minutes and finally turned to look at her with an answer out of context.

- Do they sell wine in the cafeteria? It's past noon. Today we did extend ourselves quite a bit in our talk. It would not be bad to make a toast to our Tuesdays together.

- Came? What does that have to do with my question? – Megan snapped, a little annoyed at feeling little attention.

Bastián took a few minutes again to answer. He looked out the window at the landscape completely whitened by snow. She drank the last sip of her coffee, took a deep breath, looked into her beautiful blue eyes, pursed her mouth, and just at that moment the background music was playing a song by Carla Morrison that reminded her every Tuesday.

"Come back soon to me,

I no longer understand anything about myself

You are so vital to me

Don't you understand that I feel like dying?

Return to my skin soon..."

- I think I need a little wine to clarify my answer? Megan interrupted him in his thoughts.

- Clarify? Better tell me you don't want to answer. Of course they sell wine here. We have the best in the world: Chilean Carmenere grape.

- I could not say which is the best, I have only drunk the wine made in the last season, when I feel a bit cold or after a very suffocating day. You could ask me for a drink while I go to the bathroom.

He was sweating quite a bit, despite the intense cold. In the bathroom, he sprayed some water on his head, while a thousand images flashed through his head. He returned slowly to the table and the first thing he did was take a long sip of the wine and stared at her.

- You're right, it's delicious. - Bastián told him feeling a little relieved.

- And then, tell me, why do you want to know the end date of your contract here at the station?

- The truth: I had never thought about that, but in recent months there is something that does not stop overwhelming me and I often think about that date involuntarily.

- What is it that overwhelms you?

- I thought I would spend my whole life working at the station, but for some time now, since we said goodbye at the side entrance of the cafeteria and you get lost behind the horizon of the window of that door, my mind works automatically because I really know is paralyzed at the last moment of your gaze. I can go eat and I do it mechanically. I sleep at night and at dawn I get up after dreaming of your green eyes, and so on. I cannot get you out of my thoughts for a moment, not for a single second. I know this will seem crazy to you and I am very sorry to tell you. Look at me: I'm shaking, but before we say goodbye, I just want you to think, if at some point we could try to be more than friends? Don't answer me right now, think about it and tell me, please.

Chapter 9

She snatched his glass unexpectedly. She took a sip as she stared at him, in a very different way than the times they had shared as friends.

- I don't need to think about it, Bastián, my life is here at the station- Bastián's face was stunned when Megan threw those words -. However, I also want to be with you, and I spend my time wishing every week that I arrived on Tuesday to see each other and talk.

Bastián's face flushed red with an indescribable emotion. His body was sweating, while a pleasant tingle passed through his hands and legs. Even more so when she got up from the table and walked over to him where he was sitting. He brought his lips closer to touch hers and felt how her body radiated joy. It was a torrent of emotions that he could not explain, but it circulated without brake for each part. She returned to her place and ordered two more glasses of wine to celebrate their first kiss.

Tuesdays from that day on were no longer for talking about trivial things, about each other's tasks at the station or smoothing things over after their first disastrous encounter. Now the talks were couples. There was confidence in discussing any issue, like the one Megan put on the table that Tuesday in April.

- Have you ever made love?

Bastián shuddered to the point of silence and only managed to stammer:

- Don't know. At least since I arrived at the station, two years ago, I haven't, but from my previous life, I don't remember anything. Have you done it?

At the question, Megan blushed, but recovered to answer:

- I do not know too. The same thing happens to me as to you, but for at least six months since I arrived at the station I haven't been with anyone.

Bastián knew that he could make her blush and control her emotions, so taking advantage of the security that delving into these topics gave him, he lashed out with terrible force:

- And would you like to do it with me?

Bastián had never seen her so flushed. He brought her a glass of water with his right hand, which he drank quickly. Megan's response, however, would surprise you:

- I'd love to!

A fraction of seconds later, Bastián was the one blushing and he didn't allow her to want it. There was a deep silence. They both drank some wine and relaxed on the velvety cafeteria chairs. They stared at each other waiting for someone to take the next step.

- And if we try it next Tuesday? - Bastián said with a trembling voice and dying of nerves. I felt like I was going to explode at every word that I exchanged with Megan about these intimate topics.

- What if we do it here in front of everyone, and we charge for the show? – She broke the tension, and they both burst out laughing.

- Can you go to my station at night? - proposed a more self-confident Bastián.

- You know that's complicated. Your station is one of the most controlled in the place. The best option would be to meet here in the cafeteria in the evening. In this place I have access to anywhere and after eleven at night everyone sleeps in the rest area.

- And how would I get here?

Megan gave Bastián a duplicate of his card so that he could access all the anterooms on his way to the cafeteria. Both did not stop looking at each other for a single moment. So many scenes passed through his mind that he was dying because next Tuesday would arrive.

- At twelve I'll see you here next Tuesday, Bastián.

- I'll see you at twelve, Megan.

They hugged goodbye and kissing him on the cheek, Megan moved her mouth to kiss half of his lips. Bastián went back to his station remembering that light kiss, which, although it had only been a half touch, that moment often passed through his head like the day he gave Megan his first kiss.

Chapter 10

The agreed time arrived. Bastián finished his work at the station early and immediately went to his room to shower and try to look pleasant in Megan's eyes. For the first time, he used that wood-smelling lotion that every two months was given as a gift in *Jabón de Almas* to each member of the station. He wanted to impregnate his entire body with that subtle aroma that evoked the trees of the field. He arrived half an hour early at the cafeteria. Megan had agreed to leave the air conditioning on in case she was late.

Bastián sat in the leather armchair at the back of the cafeteria. How many things had he imagined about that soft brown texture.

Megan entered the cafeteria at twelve o'clock and Bastian shuddered. She was wearing a very short shiny burgundy dress. Each of their silhouettes were perfectly appreciated. His thick legs imposed that way of walking, a bit of his straight hair fell over his beautiful sharp nose and his lips tinted with an intense red left Bastián paralyzed in the armchair, expressionless, while Megan locked the cafeteria so that no one enter to. He went to the music player and played very softly that famous genre of music from the last century relaunched a few decades ago, played acoustically by an African string instrument called the Kora, accompanied by subtle percussion. She chose her favorite 1980s hit song, *Eyes Without a Face* , originally sung by *Billy Idol* . The new version was a sultry female voice. It coincidentally evoked the moment, since in the dark what stood out the most were his eyes shining in the night.

Bastián was a sea of nerves, since before Megan's arrival. Feeling her lips, biting hers softly, she didn't know what to do, whether to first unbutton her dress little by little or lower her panties from between the dress, which might annoy her because of her desperation to be inside her. I felt that I should be calm. His desire to be with her made him impulsive. When he put his fingertips on the smooth skin of her legs, he felt her melt. It looked like a civil war, where they both exchanged riotous barrages of kisses, releasing pure heavy artillery, while clenching their buttocks and disrespectfully ripping off their underwear to expose themselves to him. They both felt how time stopped and even the music stopped listening to feel every inch of him entering until he reached, not only to the bottom of his body, but of his soul. The physical sensation was one of ecstasy, but both felt something inexplicable as they slowly merged and each movement intensified each emotion towards each other, until Bastian could not resist Megan, moving sitting in front of him, with her legs to the side. She tried for a couple of seconds, she wanted it, but she couldn't contain it and she exploded helplessly, feeling the most beautiful pleasure of her life. With that last movement, Megan also managed to reach a forced climax and threw herself exhausted to the side of the chair. Bastián's kisses wanting to devour her had excited her, as she had never imagined. They both lay there minutes later, exhausted, but happy, their legs entwined with their hands and their hair disheveled from various parts of Bastián's chest.

They were like that without issuing a single word for almost twenty minutes, even Bastián seemed sleepy at times due to physical exhaustion. He felt more tired than in his grueling sixteen-hour days at the station. Here he had worn himself out physically, emotionally, and mentally.

They didn't let go of each other's hands all that time until Megan's free left hand began to run all the way up Bastian's arm, reaching up to his chest and slowly going down to his waist.

They both turned and stared at each other. That was the understood signal that the truce was over and the volley of kisses and caresses resumed, but now he more confidently took her wrists and placed himself on top of her. He kissed her slowly and his movements inside her were just as leisurely until a moment when he began to slide rapidly and end up exhausted again on her chest. The ritual was the same throughout the night, resting sleepily for a while and then kissing again as if there wasn't another day to do it. They made love two more times until, drowsy on the couch, the first rays of dawn began to warm their eyelids. They both got dressed quickly, without saying a single word. They had such a strong commitment to their work that they went directly to their areas, tired, but motivated by having been together for the first time. They did their chores for the day with those few minutes of rest. Despite not having rested at night, the motivation of that first time made Bastián work hard, as if he had slept perfectly and showed colossal strength in the required tasks. For her part, Megan was more alert than ever. He seemed to have slept for hours, yet he had not closed his eyelids in twenty-four hours.

Chapter 11

Tuesdays had become coffee in the morning and exhausting passion at night. It was the most anticipated day for both of them, while they worked hard during the other six days to not leave any pending and to be able to concentrate on what was most important to them at that moment, loving each other.

Just as elementary school students look forward to the Friday before two days of leisure and fun. For Megan and Bastián, on Monday nights they lived the overflowing emotion of waiting for the next rays of dawn on Tuesday.

Eleven months of endless happiness passed. It was a few days away from their first anniversary. Bastián racked his brains trying to imagine a special gift for her. First he decided to write with his own blood the verses that came out of his fist, in love with Megan. He could write hundreds of them for her. What's more, he did nothing more than write down in an old notebook hidden in his drawer every sentence that came out of his soul.

On the Tuesday of their anniversary, she used that fragrance that she had never opened, and sprayed it all over her body. He cleaned himself several times. Every cell of her body vibrated from just remembering the fifty-two Tuesdays lived with her. He had a notebook where he wrote down each experience of the week. He leafed through it a little before so as not to forget any detail of it. Favourite colour blue. Wine: Carmenère. Birthday date: February 23. Favorite food: pancakes from the cafeteria. Favorite song:

Eyes without a face (Eyes without a face). He headed for the cafeteria as soon as midnight was approaching.

He began to walk, while remembering each day and moment lived with her. It arrived twenty minutes before the agreed time. He couldn't contain the desire to hug her and tell her that he wanted to be with her forever.

It was passing through a path full of red rose petals. His heart was racing with each step he took in the light of the scented candles, flooding the place with his essence. He felt the softness of the chair, where they had always made love. Soft music was heard from the player. He was trying to remember a song, but he couldn't. It was *Raw* , by Raphael. A glass of red wine was served on the table, with a yellow note: "I left you this glass so that you can begin our celebration as soon as I arrive and you drink me."

Those words made him get more excited than he already was, even excited. He took the glass feeling immensely happy and enjoyed the fresh aroma of that elixir, and with the background music he took a sip of Bordeaux, delicious, served from Megan's hands. The rest he drank in one gulp. He made himself comfortable in the chair to wait for her to enter. He was impatient to see her hair fly in the wind, through the window of it.

Inside his pants pocket he had kept a ring that he had forged every night outside his room at the station, with all the beautiful stones he had found in the vicinity.

Some more wine was poured. He had not drunk anything more delicious since he arrived at the station. He felt a little drowsy and closed his eyes for a moment.

Chapter 12

He opened his eyes, with the sensation of having fallen asleep for an instant, and he immediately tried to get up from the chair so as not to fall asleep. He felt a strong and painful pull on his left hand that even cut a part of his skin. His right hand was tied with a metal wire, when he tried to remove it with his left he felt another strong pull on his wrist. He was tied by both hands. His concern faded when he opened his eyes and could see Megan's silhouette. The music was no longer playing and there was only an aroma of alcohol like that of a hospital. He also had a very bitter taste in his mouth and an immense thirst.

- Shall we play something wicked tonight to celebrate our anniversary? – Bastian managed to ask and she smiled.

- Of course, Bastian. Today we will play something that will fascinate you, my love - he told her as he turned his back on her and began to take what looked like cutlery on the table. She was wearing a beautiful white dress, with a neckline that exposed her smooth back.

- I love kissing your back Megan- Bastián commented as he observed every millimeter of her perfect body. He was a bit sleepy and not knowing yet why he couldn't concentrate.

- I know my love, all my life you have told me: there is nothing more exciting for you than kissing my back.

Bastián was surprised to hear her.

- Lifetime? I never told you, Megan, could it be that you dreamed it?

Bastian tried to ignore Megan's statement, but his blood boiled a little at the thought that she was confusing him with someone else. It infuriated him at the thought that she might be with someone else.

- Yes, my love, all my life. Since we crossed paths one winter through the icy streets of Paris.

Bastian began to worry about Megan's delusions. I thought she was drunk or perhaps she had taken some drug, although her countenance was totally lucid.

Megan turned up the volume of the music a bit, drank a glass of wine of a different color than Bastián had drunk, opened her bag to extract an old mahogany frame with a photo inside of the beach with an incredible sunset of the horizon . The song *Hello, by Adele,* was playing on the player. She took her glass and poured another for Bastián and brought her as close as she could to high-five them and toast despite the fact that her hands were tied.

- I can almost feel the heat of that summer and the sea breeze on my skin when I see this image. My body trembles again from feeling the hot sand on my feet contrasting with the end of the waves cooling them when they reach us. Do you remember Bastian?

Everything was already confusing for Bastián, he could barely see the photo clearly due to the effect of that glass that left him lying on the chair, he didn't know how long he would be like this.

He concentrated on the scene to try to recognize each of the characters on the postcard. First she saw what she had described as the horizon in the background, with the sun setting over the sea. A clear sand, like the Mexican Caribbean, some beach in Cancun. thought. In the beautiful print, a beautiful woman was appreciated, with thick legs, perfectly tanned. Her shoulder length hair and a red bathing suit. To one side was a man in a blue bathing suit, a small yellow plastic shovel, and a cap from the Mexican soccer team. They both held, sitting on the sand, a beautiful baby with blue eyes, dressed in turquoise and splashed on the face by the sand. In his other hand he held a plastic rake. A sandcastle was the center of the image. After seeing, still a little drowsy, the photo in general, he was able to go like a camera lens sharpening and sharpening the image before his eyes. The scruffy beard of the man on the beach made it difficult to distinguish his identity, but each feature made him unmistakable. It was then that he stared at the woman in the image, but now with a different hair color, years younger, without a single wrinkle, a perfect face despite the sun and sand, but above all, every gesture of that incomparable smile. He immediately paled, he had never felt that cold combined with a frightening vibration that ran through his entire body, he could barely pronounce with drooping lips:

- Is it you and me?, Megan.

Despite having recognized the protagonists of the postcard, for a moment he thought that perhaps it was a portrait made by her to commemorate a year of relationship and the baby was probably good news for him or a fervent wish for her.

- Yes, just when we were happiest.

It was the past tense of his statement that made Bastián even more tense. He was sweating while feeling intense cold, so much so that he could barely move.

- We were? Bastián spoke slowly. I am immensely happy with you, Megan.

Bastián tried to extract the ring from his bag, but he couldn't: his hands were tied.

- Are you looking for this, Emanuel?

Bastián's face fell even more when he saw how Megan was holding the ring that she forged with so much sacrifice, and, furthermore, throwing it to the floor with contempt.

- You have to try harder. This nonsense won't make me come back to you.

Bastián was a sea of confusion, and a torrent of tears began to flow down his cheeks when he saw the gift he had prepared for Megan roll on the floor.

- I'm Bastian, Megan. You're confusing me.

- No, dear, that's your real name.

Megan's smile was no longer cute. It conveyed terror. It was unrecognizable to Bastian.

- That's not my name, Megan. You know my name, Bastian. You've screamed it in my ear when we make love here every Tuesday night. Remember it! How can you forget it?

- It is the lie that they wanted to fabricate in this horrible purgatory of shit called *Jabón de Almas* . You are not Bastián, the tireless, the altruistic, the one who watches over the lives of others, the one who would take off his shirt for his neighbor. You are Emanuel, the ruthless killer I fell in love with when I was almost a child.

Bastian began to cry. He wouldn't stop sobbing. Some of Megan's words echoed in his mind and he didn't know why.

-Megan, I have never killed anyone.

- You murdered the person we loved the most in life and with that you also killed me. I never lived again, I just studied and worked tirelessly to get here. I lived each day of my life thinking about being right here, close to you.

Bastián looked at the photo once more and when he saw the helpless baby he started crying.

- Are you sure? – Bastián pronounced as if beginning to believe in the possibility that everything Megan said was true because he had no idea what had happened in his previous life, where he had committed a crime without knowing what it was, but that was why he was in *Soap of souls* suffering for their deeds.

- So sure that I was when you arrived drunk and drugged that night and shouting that it was not your son -Megan cried intensely-. And I came here to ask you, why did you do it, Bastián? Why did you end up with what we loved the most?

- It wasn't me, Megan, I swear, I've never been to the beach – Bastián refuted, trying to shield himself, but he knew that Megan's words were true because just when he was narrating what had happened he remembered that tender and angelic look from blue eyes on hers.

- You had never behaved like this, but that night we argued and you decided to go to the bar to get drunk and then you argued in your defense that a homeless man offered you "a very strong drug that would fascinate you." And you ruined our lives for all of us. I followed your sentence and the place where you would come. I changed my identity to access here. I even had to commit some crime to see you suffer like you did, while you drowned Mau in the sea.

- I couldn't have done that Megan. I can't even imagine it. My soul doesn't have that kind of evil.

- I would like to think that this is true, that this horrendous place works, that the *Soap of Souls* can really clean the most sinister in each person, but every night I cannot sleep remembering our son and how you ripped him out of our lives when we were so happy .

Bastián did not stop crying.

- Megan, forgive me!

Bastián sobbed, while she opened her bag to extract a scalpel with which she began to slowly cut each part of Bastián's body. She wanted to see him suffer as much as she had suffered for the past few years and still she wouldn't reach his full pain to ease hers.

He had taken away what he loved most. There is no greater love than that of a mother for her son and he ended that bond.

- That wasn't me. I am no longer that person that you say. I'm Bastián and I've never killed someone - Bastián held back his tears a little and before Megan's cuts he held back any cry of pain. Do with me what you want. I'm not that person, but if I did something like that, I'm not worth living either.

- In the trial you claimed that you had received a message, when you were drinking, that made you doubt me and you wanted to hurt me as much as you felt.

Megan continued to cut Bastián's lying body, who only cried with sadness, but not with pain. The torture to which he was subjected was not compared to the internal suffering for the atrocity committed.

.   -You're right, I deserve it; End my life, Megan.

Those words hit rock bottom in Megan. At that moment he was cutting part of Bastián's belly with the scalpel and he stopped for a moment when he thought about his son, about what he had experienced with Emanuel. At that time she would become a murderer like him.

Seeing him destroyed, full of blood and without strength, she thought that his pain was not comparable to hers, but killing him meant being the same as him, and above all else, even though she did not want to accept it, killing another person, one who rose with the light of dawn to give their best effort for humanity. He was no longer Emanuel, he was Bastián, the man who, despite his performance, had made her feel in love.

Nor could she repair the damage to Bastián, and wrapped in a sea of confused thoughts, she ran out of the place and moved away forever.

He left Bastián's life in God's hands while he slowly bled to death in the cafeteria. He would probably die within hours from his injuries and thus neither God would have absolved his grief nor Megan's.

Chapter 13

Only the sound of the pulsations could be heard on the monitor in that hospital room.

He awoke in a closed place of immense proportions. It was like a colossal warehouse, brilliant white radiating light. In each cardinal point there was a word and an illuminated path led to each one. Happiness, health, love and success were the words.

Bastián assured that he had self-inflicted the injuries for which he lay in a bed in the main hospital of the *Jabón de Almas stations* . As incredible as his version seemed, he limited himself to not giving any more testimony and the case ended there, despite so many doubts as to how he had managed to do it if he was handcuffed and how he had access to so many places in Jabón de Almas to get to the *basement* of Cafeteria. He just repeated over and over again: "I did all that. I deserved it for the sins I may have committed in my previous life."

He had miraculously saved his life thanks to the fact that the cleaner of the place forgot his belongings and returned to look for them after midnight. In his mind he only wanted, despite the wounds and the impossibility of healing them, especially those of the soul, to see Megan again, but he didn't even know her real name.

Bastián was acquitted from *Jabón de Almas* prematurely for his high performance at the station. Twenty-seven months he remained there so that he could rehabilitate and recover physically in the best way in the place where he wanted.

Near the sea, there between waves, every day he asked for forgiveness for what he had done, while he let go of each of the letters written to Megan that when wet with salt water the ink disappeared, and in the end he let go of the last poetry he had written. wrote to him.

"Your look gave you away the moment we saw each other for the first time
He looked at me like he's been there forever
like it never shined without me
as if we were born together
And learned to walk and love hand in hand.
staring down on me declared,
That your heart was meant to be mine
and that your clean soul would lie next to mine.

Megan, for her part, had been happy again thousands of kilometers from Bastian. One of the reasons why she didn't kill him that night was because just when she saw him bleed to death, in her belly she felt that dizziness and nausea from a few years ago, that unique sensation that women can identify. Life had given him back what he lost, the result of that fictitious love with Bastián at the station. Never, not even by mistake, would he think of being with someone else and running the risk of losing what he loved the most.

Bastián swore to look for Megan, and despite being able to choose the place where he could rebuild his life, he only wanted to be in that one place where he could not be, because he did not know how to get there and where he would not be welcome either, in Megan's heart .

End